MARCEL
HOLLYW

1 Marcel and Céline are French mice. (Marcel is a detective and Céline is a painter.) One summer they go to Los Angeles on holiday.

2 They take a bus from the airport to Hollywood.

3 Céline looks at the map.

4 They walk to Maytree Avenue. Then...

5

Number 28 – this is it.

Do you want to know about the Waldmans? This says: 'Arnold is a film director, and Claudia comes from Italy.'

Their daughter Lois, is fifteen years old....

6 Marcel opens the door and goes in.

Look, Céline There's the door to our holiday flat.

The photos in *Hollywood Holidays* were right.

Yes, this is Beautiful.

7 At ten o'clock Marcel and Céline go to bed. But at twelve o'clock Marcel opens his eyes again. He can hear a noise.

8 He goes upstairs to the kitchen.

Then he sees a note.

10 In the morning, Arnold and Claudia Waldman read the note, too.

11 The Waldmans talk for a long time. Then at 9.15 Arnold leaves for his office. Marcel and Céline go, too.

12 Arnold drives to the Silver Star Film Studios.

13 At 9.45.

14 In his office, the film director walks up and down.

15 The telephone rings. Arnold answers it.

16 Céline looks at Marcel.

17

18 Arnold leaves his office at 10.15. Marcel and Céline go, too.
First he goes shopping and buys a suitcase. After that he goes to his bank and puts $1 million in the suitcase. Then he drives to Long Beach. At 11.55...

19 Arnold finds room 309 on the Queen Mary. A man with red hair opens the door to him.

Arnold Waldman?

Yes, that's me.

That's a big ship!

Ssshh!

20 Suddenly ...

It's all there. Now – where's my daughter? Is she OK?

Yes, she's OK... now. But this is only the first million. You don't get her back today.

21

The first million! But I...

Get out, Waldman! Go home. Wait near the telephone.

What do we do? Go with Arnold or stay here?

Let's stay with the kidnapper.

22 Arnold leaves. Then the kidnapper telephones a friend.

Chuck? It's me, Stan. Yes, I have the money and I'm leaving now.

Get in here. Quick!

23 At 2.15.

24 At 6.30 the car stops at an old house.
Marcel looks at Céline. Céline looks at Marcel.
It's very quiet. Then Stan takes the suitcase into the house.

25 He puts the suitcase on the table and opens it. 'Look at that!' says Chuck. The two men smile, but they don't look *under* the money. They go into the kitchen.

26 At eleven o'clock Stan and Chuck are sleeping. Then...

27 Marcel and Céline find Lois in a small bedroom. She's on the bed and she can't move.

28 Marcel and Céline go downstairs again. Then...

29 Very quietly, Marcel gives the guns to Céline.

30 Then, Marcel and Céline take the telephone upstairs.

31 In the bathroom, Marcel telephones the police.

34 Marcel and Céline walk to a bus-stop near the house. They wait there. They wait and wait. No buses come. 'It's very early in the morning,' says Marcel. Then he looks across the road and sees a big lorry.

35 Later...

He and Céline run to the lorry and get on it.

36 The lorry stops near Sunset Boulevard. From there, Marcel and Céline walk to 28 Maytree Avenue. They eat some fruit and drink a lot of coffee. Then...

37 Lois talks to the TV and newspaper people. Marcel and Céline watch. But only for a short time. Then they swim in the Waldmans' pool.

Of course they are happy. It's hot... The sky is blue... And they *are* in Hollywood!

ACTIVITIES

Before you read

1 Look at the pictures in 'Marcel Goes To Hollywood.'

   a In which pictures can you see:

   a *suitcase?* a *gun?* a *map?* a *lorry?* a *note?* a *ship?*

   Find the words in your dictionary.

   b What are these words in your language?

   avenue bathroom detective film director kidnapper
   mice a million painter pool studio to ring to leave
   downstairs upstairs

   c What is the story about?

After you read

2 Finish these sentences about the story.

   DAY 1: Marcel and Céline arrive in Los Angeles.

   a First...

   b At ten o'clock ...

   DAY 2:

   c At 8.45 in the morning ...

   d At 9.45 ...

   e At twelve o'clock ...

   f At 6.30 in the evening ...

   g At eleven o'clock ...

   h At twelve o'clock ...

Writing

3 Write a letter from Marcel or Céline to a friend in Paris.

4 What do the newspapers say about Lois? Write the story.

River Gelt

"I leap with my primeval ble
down wild ra

W. H. Do

River Gelt

2

Gelt Woods and Greenwell

Most of the woodland in the vicinity of the river Gelt has been designated a Site of Special Scientific Interest. The woods are an important example of gorge woodland of a type peculiar to northern Cumbria and parts of Scotland, with a rich mix of native trees including sessile oak, hairy and silver birch, rowan, holly and hazel. Some areas were clear felled after the Second World War and planted up with larch, Scots pine and other conifers.

The name Gelt may have derived from an Irish word meaning 'wild', brought to the area via Ireland by migrating Norse settlers, but it could also be a variation of the Gaelic word 'galt' meaning 'magic'. Rising in the Pennines above Castle Carrock there is, perhaps, something about the river Gelt's journey through this rocky landscape that is both wild and magical.

rowan

rocks
in the heart of no man's wood!"

3

To follow this walk route, turn left out of the car park, across the road bridge over the river Gelt and left at the road junction. Follow the road up hill a short distance and turn left along a footpath signposted to Tow Top.

This track is known as Thief Street, probably because it was used 500 years ago as an escape route by border raiders hiding stolen cattle in the woods. Known as the Reivers these raiders were the renegade families, resident throughout the Scottish / English border at that time, who terrorised each other and their more law-abiding neighbours with their ruthless lifestyle of violence, robbery and blackmail. 'Reive' is an old dialect word meaning 'to plunder' and the word 'bereaved' derives from the fact that a visit by the Reivers invariably left some of their victims dead.

Go through the kissing-gate and follow the wide track on the left edge of the field, with the sand quarry over to your left and the moto-cross tracks on the rounded hill ahead over to the right. Go through another kissing gate through an area of gorse and broom.

This is good habitat for birds such as linnets and yellowhammers.

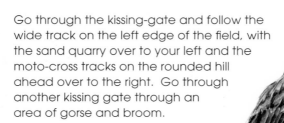

yellowhammer on gorse

illustration based on © image
Philip Newman (rspb-images.com)

Thief Street

Keep straight on to a third kissing-gate and continue up hill.

Flowers to be found here during the course of the summer season include foxglove, wood anemone, wood sorrel, and red campion.

At the cross tracks go straight ahead along a narrow hedged track and then over a stile.

The wooded hill to the left is called 'Watch Hill' and may well have been a look-out point for the fugitive Reivers just as the deep, wooded hollow in the woods to the right, called Peck O' Big Hole, might have concealed hundreds of stolen cattle. Buzzards are regularly seen overhead, gliding on air thermals, and the woods provide a plentiful supply of food for small birds like long-tailed tits, blue tits and chiffchaffs. The raucous calling of jays is often heard in these woods.

foxglove

rievers lino print for bronze panel

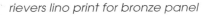

6

jay
illustration based on © image
Mike Lane (rspb-images.com)

Go over a stile at the next path junction, along a narrow
fenced footpath; continue to the next stile and into a
field where you walk along the left boundary, alongside
a narrow plantation.

>The trees here include Douglas fir,
>Lodgepole pine and Scots pine.

Cross over the next stile into a second field and keep to
the left.

>Open farmland adjacent to the woodland
>edge provides suitable terrain for lapwing,
>curlew and both the great spotted and
>green woodpecker.

At the field end, cross over the stile onto a shady track,
which takes you to a road where you turn left. After
about 90 metres, turn right along the Public Bridleway
signposted to Greenwell.

view towards Geltsdale

8

You get glimpses of the Pennine ridge as you walk down the lonning and you will see a rich array of ferns, honeysuckle and ivy on the walls. Ivy is a particularly valuable source of winter food for wild birds and insects as it produces its flowers in October and then fruits in the New Year.

Go over the railway bridge.

The railway-cutting below, on the Newcastle – Carlisle line, was excavated in the 1830's and is nearly two kilometres long and up to 34 metres deep.

Pass through the gate and follow the grassy track to your left. After about 90 metres, the path turns right along the edge of the field and continues until you come to another road.

Cross the road and go through the gate along the lane opposite, which goes to Greenwell.

The land either side provides some excellent habitats for wildlife, with a mix of bracken and scrub woodland on the slope to the right and some marshy areas below on the left. Watch out for roe deer, the smallest of our native deer.

Carry on along the lane past a bridleway signpost and a large silver birch tree on the right.

The birch tree is festooned with twiggy clumps, commonly called 'witches' brooms', which are caused by a parasitic fungus.

Our route turns left over the stone stile onto the footpath signposted to Middle Gelt, just before you come into the small hamlet of Greenwell.

It is well worth pausing for a few minutes in this peaceful little oasis, which seems to have been left behind by time. There used to be a working water mill here, now a private house, and you will see the old mill-race, a stone lined channel that once carried the water to the mill's wheel.

Continue your walk along the path signposted to Middle Gelt, through a marshy field alongside a fence on your right and over a wooden step-stile into another field, where you join the river Gelt three kilometres upstream from where you started.

dipper

illustration based on © image
Mike Lane (rspb-images.com)

Greenwell

Two birds typical of upland rivers can be seen along here. The dipper, notable for its ability to walk under water collecting insects from the river bottom, and the grey wagtail with its distinctive wagging tail.

Follow the bank of the river downstream to the far end of this long field, which used to be three fields, where you rather unexpectedly arrive at a gas-terminal enclosure. Keep to the right of this enclosure and cross another stile into the woods before turning right onto the road at Middle Gelt.

Middle Gelt viaduct - detail of stonework

The railway viaduct towering 17 metres overhead was built in 1835 and is one of the earliest examples of a 'skew' bridge, where the arches are constructed with angled stonework. It is said that the builder first calculated the angles using a model made with pieces of turnip. The road bridge was built in 1723 and widened in 1867.

Turn right over the bridge then left through a gate into Gelt Woods.

This part of the woods is managed by the Royal Society for the Protection of Birds. The scrub, on the left, is being encouraged to provide a habitat for summer migrant birds including the chiffchaff and garden warbler, and shallow pools have been dug out in the wet ground for frogs and toads. Forty years ago, the original native trees were felled in large parts of Gelt Woods and replaced with conifers to provide a quick-growing crop of timber. Now the RSPB is gradually removing them to facilitate a naturally regenerated return to native woodland which will be more compatible with indigenous wildlife.

After a while, the path climbs away from this fast-flowing section of river, through one of the remaining conifer areas and then descends again to a calmer stretch. Cross the bridge over Hell Beck and ascend the steps up the steep slope to a more gradual incline away from the river, curving away to the left below.

This half of the wood is owned by Brampton Parish Council.

Follow the path as it meanders through the trees to a bend overlooking the river again, where you bear right and then left.

The half-sphere-shaped sculpture perched on the left was carved from a solid piece of elm by the artist Keith Barrett. It was commissioned some years ago by Brampton Parish Council, as part of a community sculpture project.

wych elm

elm sculpture

The spectacular cliff-face is an old quarry, excavated over several centuries, first by the Romans and more recently by local people who had commoners' rights to quarry here in what was once the Brampton Freestone Quarry. Many of the buildings in Brampton were constructed with stone extracted from the Gelt Woods area.

quarry face

Soft yielding water overcomes the hard rock
Low flowing river overcomes the high crag

The stone and timber seat tucked away, behind the brow, in front of the cliff was made by the sculptor Vivien Mousdell. The text is taken from an ancient Chinese Taoist manuscript in which the human journey through life is compared with that of a river through a rocky landscape.

Down by the river there is a bird-watching hide based on a Celtic roundhouse design and made from locally harvested oak, hazel, willow and bracken.

Continue along the path uphill for a short stretch and then descend past several smaller quarried cliffs, where you take the left fork down to the river, along a stone causeway with another section of higher cliffs rising up to your right.

bird hide

sculpture seat by Vivien Mousdell

Near the top, there are some roughly-carved Roman numerals dating from when the Romans quarried stone here to build Hadrian's Wall. Due to erosion, the cliffs are very dangerous and the inscriptions inaccessible. The damp sandstone facilitates a profusion of rare mosses, ferns and liverworts and an abundance of flowering plants, such as golden saxifrage.

ferns and liverworts

golden saxifrage

20

Woodland in the Eden catchment

Gelt Woods are one of very few surviving ancient native woods in East Cumbria. About 7000 years ago, when our climate was warmer and humans had made very little impact on the natural landscape, something like two thirds of the British Isles were covered in dense woodland. The only areas clear of trees were high mountains and extensive tracts of low lying wetland.

Left to its own devices and given enough time and space, a wood will quite naturally generate a huge variety of habitats ranging from open, sunlit glades to impenetrable thickets. Most of our wild mammals, two thirds of our breeding birds, more than half of our butterflies and moths and one sixth of our flowering plants are dependent on woodland.

Almost nothing remains of the original uninterrupted woodland wilderness although there are pockets of what is called primary woodland where the trees have been felled over hundreds of years but the woodland has never been clear felled. This means that all the diverse components relating to the woodland's ecological interdependency and continuity survive.

Some of the best examples of semi-natural woodland around the Eden catchment region are to be found in gorges and gills, in close proximity to rivers and streams, where steep ground has prohibited agricultural improvement.

potholes

22

This stretch of the river provides an impressive example of how fast-flowing water can cut its way through stone.

Carry on alongside the river until you get to a stand of tall, thin conifers and beech trees. Leave the main path and walk to a bench on the left.

On the opposite bank of the river you will see a collection of potholes worn into the sandstone by pebbles spinning around in whirlpools when the river is in full spate.

Return to the path and continue up the slope away from the river. Bear left at the top and back down to the river again.

beech and beech-masts

bracken thatch

The variety of trees in this area includes hornbeam, oak, cherry and sweet chestnut. Birds you might see include spring migrants such as blackcaps, woodwarblers and redstarts. Another observation-hide provides an ideal vantage point for watching birds.

Continue to Low Gelt Bridge to complete the walk.

Powterneth Beck runs into the River Gelt here and the Gelt continues flowing west for another three kilometres before it joins the River Irthing, which in turn joins the River Eden just north of Warwick Bridge.

redstart

illustration based on © image
Mark Hamblin (rspb-images.com)

24